Magic Ballerina

Delphie and the Magic Spell

AND

Rosa and the Golden Bird

Welcome to the world of Enchantia!

I have always loved to dance. The captivating music and wonderful stories of ballet are so inspiring. So come with me and let's follow Delphie and Rosa on their magical adventures in Enchantia, where the stories of dance will take you on a very special journey.

DISCARDED

p.s. Turn to the end of each story to learn a special dance step from me...

Special thanks to
Linda Chapman, Katie May
and Nellie Ryan

Delphie and the Magic Spell first published in paperback in Great Britain by
HarperCollins *Children's Books* in 2008
Rosa and the Golden Bird first published in paperback in Great Britain by
HarperCollins *Children's Books* in 2009
Published together in this two-in-one edition in 2011
HarperCollins *Children's Books* is a division of HarperCollins *Publishers* Ltd,
77-85 Fulham Palace Road, Hammersmith, London W6 8JB

The HarperCollins website address is
www.harpercollins.co.uk

1

Text copyright © HarperCollins *Children's Books* 2008, 2009
Illustrations copyright © HarperCollins *Children's Books* 2008, 2009

MAGIC BALLERINA™ and the 'Magic Ballerina' logo are
trademarks of HarperCollins Publishers Ltd.

ISBN 978-0-00-741441-3

Printed and bound in England by
Clays Ltd, St Ives plc

Mixed Sources
Product group from well-managed
forests and other controlled sources
www.fsc.org Cert no. SW-COC-1806
© 1996 Forest Stewardship Council
FSC

FSC is a non-profit international organisation established to promote the
responsible management of the world's forests. Products carrying the FSC
label are independently certified to assure consumers that they come
from forests that are managed to meet the social, economic and
ecological needs of present and future generations.

Find out more about HarperCollins and the environment at
www.harpercollins.co.uk/green

Magic Ballerina™
Delphie and the Magic Spell

Darcey Bussell

HarperCollins *Children's Books*

ENCH
Royal Palace
Sugar Plum Fairy's Cottage
The Village
The Land of SWEETS
THEATRE
Theatre

To Phoebe and Zoe, as they are the inspiration behind Magic Ballerina.

Contents

Prologue

In the soft, pale light, the girl stood with her head bent and her hands held lightly in front of her. There was a moment's silence and then the first notes of the music began. For as long as the girl could remember music had seemed to tell her of another world – a magical, exciting world – that lay far, far away. She always felt if she could just close her eyes and lose herself, then she would get there. Maybe this time. As the music swirled inside her, she swept her arms above her head, rose on to her toes and began to dance…

The Bluebird's Dance

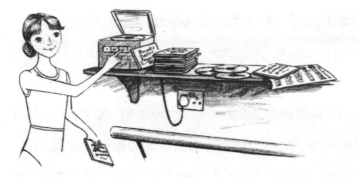

The ballet studio was quiet and still. It could only be a couple of hours since it had been full of girls dancing for their ballet teacher, Madame Za-Za. Now there was just one girl left.

Delphie Durand pressed the button on the CD player and then ran lightly to the centre of the room. She waited for the music to start, one foot slightly in front of the other, her head bent, her eyes looking down at her red ballet shoes. All the other girls in her class had pink ones but it wasn't just the colour that made Delphie's shoes different from theirs. Delphie's ballet shoes were also magic!

Madame Za-Za, the owner of the ballet school, had given them to Delphie three weeks ago. She'd told her they were very special but Delphie hadn't known just how special until two nights later when the shoes had started glowing and sparkling. When Delphie had put them on, they had whisked her away to Enchantia – a magical land where all the characters from the different ballets lived. A land full of incredible adventures!

Delphie smiled as she remembered the adventure she'd had there. It had been scary but amazing! Just then, the first few notes of the music swelled out from the CD player. Delphie quickly pushed thoughts of Enchantia to the back of her mind. She had to get this dance right.

She heard the music she had been waiting for and glided forward into a run, taking tiny steps as she skimmed across the floor. As the music changed, she stopped on her tiptoes, looking from side to side like a bird, her arms held

slightly behind her like wings. *Wait*,
Delphie told herself, listening to the music
carefully. *One, two…*

She danced forward and turned a
pirouette, before travelling forward again
and stopping with one leg held behind
her, one arm in front,
trying to look as if she
was a bird
flying. All of
Madame Za-Za's
instructions from the
class earlier ran through
her head – lift the chin…
shoulders down… keep
your back strong… turn
out that leg…

Delphie was so busy thinking about the placing of her leg that she lost her balance and stumbled. Bother! It was so hard trying to concentrate on everything at the same time. Before she had started ballet classes, she had simply danced just how she had felt. Now she was learning that you had to make sure every bit of your body was doing the right thing at the right time. But Delphie found that when she concentrated on her legs, she forgot about her arms and then she remembered them and realised her head was wrong and her shoulders were up and by the time she had got those right, her legs were wrong again.

But I've got to get it right, she thought as she walked back over to the CD player to restart the music. *There's only one day to go!*

The very next morning there were going to be auditions for the school's end of term show. It was a woodland ballet and the main part was the Bluebird. All of Delphie's class wanted to be the Bluebird. Delphie had been practising and practising.

The door to the studio opened and Delphie saw Madame Za-Za look in. A slim, elegant woman with her greying hair pulled back into a low bun, she was wearing a long floaty skirt over footless tights and a wrapover top.

"Well, Delphie?" she said. "How is it going?"

As Delphie met her teacher's gaze, she couldn't stop the truth from bursting out. "Actually, I'm not doing very well, Madame Za-Za. I just can't seem to get the

dance right no
matter how hard
I try!"

"Maybe you are
trying *too* hard,
child," Madame
Za-Za said.

Delphie frowned.
"What do you
mean?"

"It will make sense one day, Delphie,"
Madame Za-Za said with a smile. "Maybe
sooner than you imagine." And with that
she left the room.

Delphie sighed, restarted the music
and went back to the centre to try again.
But even the very first run felt wrong and

stiff as she tried to think about her feet,
arms and head all at once. She broke off
with a groan and went to stop the music
before glancing at the clock on the wall. It
was nearly time to go. Her mum and dad
would be home from work.

With a sigh, Delphie went over to the
wooden barre that ran around the edge of
the room and began to do some slow
stretching exercises. She was just finishing
when the door opened.

Delphie looked round, expecting to see
Madame Za-Za again, but in her place
stood Sukie Taylor. Delphie's heart sank.
She was in Delphie's ballet class and was
very, very good at ballet, but she didn't
seem to like Delphie at all.

Sukie looked surprised to see her. "Oh. Hi. I left something." She picked up a pink cardigan from the back of a chair and switched off the music. "What are you doing here?"

Delphie shrugged. "Just practising."

"For the auditions?" Sukie's eyes narrowed. "Well, you won't have a chance.

You've only been coming to classes for three weeks and Madame Za-Za has pretty much said that I'm going to be the Bluebird. Everyone knows I'm the best dancer in the class."

Delphie swallowed. *Just ignore her*, she told herself. She didn't want to get into an argument.

"You never know," Sukie went on. "Maybe if you try hard enough you'll get to be a rabbit or something."

Delphie watched as Sukie smirked and flounced out, then Delphie pulled a face. Sukie might think she didn't have a chance but no one would know until the actual auditions. *I might be the Bluebird*, Delphie thought hopefully. She crossed her fingers. Oh, she *so* hoped she would be. But first she just needed to get the dance right...

A Noise in the Night

"Mum, come and see this bit!" Delphie
called after supper. She was sitting on the
sofa, her feet curled under her, watching
the ballet of *Cinderella*. She had been given
the DVD for her birthday. It was her
favourite scene where the fairy godmother
changed the pumpkin and mice into a
coach and horses and then transformed

Cinderella from a servant girl in rags into a beautiful princess.

Mrs Durand came through to the lounge and sat down beside Delphie on the sofa. "Maybe one day you'll be able to dance like that," she said, stroking Delphie's long brown hair. "Wouldn't that be wonderful?"

Delphie snuggled up to her mum. "Oh yes," she breathed. There was nothing she wanted more in the world.

At bedtime, Delphie kissed her mum and dad goodnight and went upstairs. As she got into her nightdress, she looked hopefully at her red ballet shoes sitting on her desk. *Please sparkle tonight*, she willed them. *Please!*

But they looked as still as ever, just as they had every other night that week.

Every evening she had lain in bed, willing the shoes to glow, hoping to hear music in the air, just like she had the first time they had taken her to Enchantia.

It would be just so amazing to go back, Delphie thought as she got into bed, after brushing her teeth and hair. *I'd love to see Sugar the Sugar Plum Fairy again, and all the other people I met, like the Nutcracker*  *and the waltzing flowers and the dancing snowflakes.* She shivered as the image of a rat's face with red eyes, long whiskers and sharp teeth popped into her brain. The one person she wouldn't want to see again was the evil King Rat! He hated dancing and was always trying to stop it. Delphie had been to his castle and met him and his mouse guards and it had been very scary!

To try and stop thinking about it, Delphie focused on the audition the next day. She began to go through the steps of the dance in her mind, practising them over and over again, and before she knew it she was drifting off to sleep…

° ⊚ ·*· ☆ ·⊚·*· ✫ ⊚ ·*· ★ ⊚ ·*· °

Delphie's eyes blinked open. She felt sure that something had woken her. Sitting up, she glanced at her bedside clock. It was just past midnight.

Suddenly she heard a faint noise. *Music!*
As she listened it grew louder. Delphie
looked at her desk. Her red ballet shoes
were glittering and shining like rubies.
Throwing back her duvet, she jumped
out of bed and ran over to them. Did this
mean another adventure was about to
begin?

Delphie picked them up, her fingers
trembling in excitement. The first time she
had gone to Enchantia
the shoes had
whisked her off
to a theatre. Delphie
tied the ribbons
of the shoes in
anticipation.

As she tied the bows, her feet started
to tingle. She stood up and the feeling
whooshed all the way from her toes up to
her head. A second later, she was swirling
around in a myriad of colours – pink,
purple, blue, red, yellow, orange, green...

And then she landed with a bump to find
herself sitting on a red seat, in the same
darkened theatre that she had arrived at
before, only this time the air was very cold.
She shivered and rubbed the bare skin on
her arms. The stage was shut away behind
red velvet curtains. Music started playing
and the red curtains began to open.

Delphie jumped up eagerly and then
caught her breath. It was all so different. The
first time she had been here there had been

light and colour, the scenery had shown
mountains, fields and a village, as well as
King Rat's castle and there had been lots of
characters on the stage even though they had
all been asleep. But now the background
scenery was just painted white and the stage
was empty. The floor was covered in a thick
blanket of snow. There were bare trees on the
stage, their branches covered in icicles.

Delphie walked hesitantly down towards the stage. "Sugar?" Her voice echoed through the empty auditorium. She didn't like this. There was a feeling in the air as if something was horribly wrong.

"Sugar!" she called uneasily. "Where are you?"

The Glittering Palace

Just at that moment, a flash of blue zipped across the stage. Delphie's brown eyes widened as she saw a beautiful turquoise bird about the size of a robin. It landed on one of the icy branches and sang loudly, its tiny wings fluttering, its head cocked on one side.

"Hello," Delphie said, going up the steps at the side of the stage and looking at the little bird. "Do you know what's going on?"

"Yes!" the bird twittered.

Delphie was only a little bit surprised to find that it could talk. She was in Enchantia after all!

"My name's Skye," the bluebird said. "Are you Delphie?" Delphie nodded and the bird carried on. "I've been waiting for you. Sugar thought the ballet shoes might bring you here again. We're in terrible trouble, Delphie."

"Trouble? Why?" Delphie asked in alarm.

"King Rat has cast a spell over Enchantia to make it winter all the time," Skye told her. "He has a model of Enchantia sealed inside a glass globe. Whenever he shakes the globe, snow swirls around and then it falls in real life too.

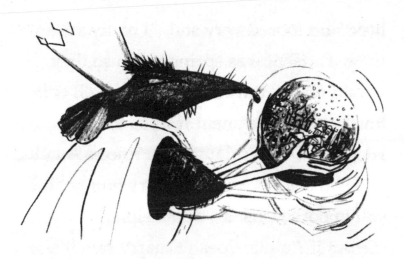

When it's as snowy and icy-cold as this no one can dance properly."

Delphie shivered as Skye continued.

"Everyone just stays indoors and all the animals and birds have either hibernated or gone away to where it is warmer. All my family have flown off. I hurt my wing though and couldn't keep up with them so I had to come back." She dipped her head and looked very sad. "I really miss them. I wish it was spring again so they would return. But King Rat says he'll only break the enchantment if he can marry the King and Queen's daughter, Princess Aurelia, and she doesn't want to marry him at all."

"I'm not surprised!" said Delphie.

"But if Aurelia doesn't marry him it's going to stay winter forever," Skye sighed. "Sugar is at the palace now, trying to comfort the princess. Do you think you might be able to help us? I can show you the way there."

"I'll try!" promised Delphie. "Let's go!"

"It's this way!" sang Skye. "Follow me!"

The bluebird flew off the stage and Delphie ran after her, finding herself in a

wood. There were tall dark trees rising up
on either side and the air was totally still
and silent apart from the sound of Skye
singing as she swooped on ahead.

Delphie ran as fast as she could.
It helped keep her warm.
Luckily her ballet shoes
didn't seem to
get wet.

"Here we are!" the bluebird called finally
as she flew out of the woods.

Delphie stopped with a gasp as she looked
up at the palace in front of them. It was made
of glittering white marble and had tall
pointed turrets, a moat that had turned to
sparkling ice and a big golden door.

"It'll be warm inside," Skye said, tapping
on the entrance with her beak.

The door opened and a large, cheerful-
looking guard looked out.

"We're here to see Sugar," Skye told him.
"I've brought Delphie, the girl with the
magic ballet shoes."

The guard beamed.
"Everyone's been hoping
you'd arrive," he said to
Delphie. "My name's
Griff. Come in! You must
be freezing out there."

"Thanks!" Delphie hurried into the castle.
Through the door was a high-ceilinged hall
with richly embroidered tapestries. There
were three huge log fires burning and the
warm air wrapped around Delphie like a hug.

"Here," Griff said, coming over with a
purple velvet cloak. "Put this on until
you've warmed up."

The material was soft and thick and Delphie pulled it snugly around her.

"I'll go and fetch the King and Queen," Griff said. "We're in awful trouble. I really hope you can help us this time."

Delphie shivered. She hoped so too.

Delphie's Plan

Griff hurried off. A few minutes later, he returned with four other people – a beautiful girl with long brown hair wearing a pink dress and a delicate silver tiara, a woman in a midnight-blue dress, a man wearing dark trousers, a gold crown and a purple fur-lined cloak and…

"Sugar!" Delphie exclaimed in delight

as she saw her friend the fairy. Sugar
looked just as she had the first time Delphie
had seen her and was wearing a pale lilac
tutu, tights and ballet shoes.

Sugar grabbed Delphie's hands and
swirled her around. "It's great to see you
again, Delphie!" They stopped and hugged
and then the smile faded from Sugar's face.
"Has Skye told you what has happened?"

Delphie nodded. "King Rat is totally evil!"

"He certainly is," said the princess,
coming forward. "I'm Princess Aurelia, and
this is my father and mother, King Tristan
and Queen Isabella of Enchantia."

"Welcome to our palace, Delphie," King
Tristan said. "It's a pleasure to meet you."

Delphie wasn't sure what to do. She had

never met a king and queen before. She
swept her leg behind her and curtseyed
gracefully, keeping her back straight, just
like she had to do at the start and end of
every ballet class. She saw Sugar's look of
approval and glowed.

Queen Isabella came forward and took her hands in hers. "I really hope you *can* help us.

"Yes," said Princess Aurelia desperately. "I don't want to marry King Rat but if it's the only way of stopping Enchantia being frozen in winter forever, then I will do it."

"Surely there must be something else we can do," said Delphie. "Can't someone just steal the globe or something?"

"We've tried," answered Sugar. "But it's impossible. King Rat won't let it out of his sight. He says that the only thing that will make him break the globe is if he marries Aurelia – today!"

"I'm going to *have* to marry him!" Princess Aurelia's eyes filled with tears. Her mother and father quickly comforted her.

Delphie's thoughts tumbled over each other. What could they do? There had to be some other way…

Suddenly there was a very loud croaking sound from just outside the window. Delphie jumped. "What's that?" she said, covering her ears as the noise came again even louder.

"Oh, that's Priscilla the toad," said Sugar. "She's been croaking like that ever since the moat froze over," said Princess Aurelia. "It's *really* annoying."

There was another loud croak. Delphie
looked out of the window. An extremely
large, extremely grumpy-looking toad
about the size of a large dog, was sitting on
the ice of the moat.

"She croaks all day and all night unless
she's eating," said the King. "It's impossible
to sleep! I wish she'd go away."

"We'll do something about her soon,
dear," said the Queen soothingly. "Maybe
Sugar can use her magic to turn her into a
nightingale or a mouse or something for
a while – anything that doesn't make
such a dreadful noise. But first we have
to decide what we are going to do about
King Rat."

The Queen's words gave Delphie an idea.

"Maybe we can do something about *both* things at the same time!" she said.

"What do you mean?" asked Princess Aurelia.

A grin spread over Delphie's face. "Sugar, could

you really use your magic to turn Priscilla the toad into something else?"

"Yes," replied Sugar, looking confused. "But what would I turn her into?"

"If you turned her into a beautiful princess – the most beautiful in the whole of Enchantia, even more beautiful than Aurelia, then I bet King Rat would want to marry her instead," said Delphie.

"Of course!" gasped Sugar but then she frowned. "But how would that solve our problem about it being winter? King Rat wouldn't have to break the enchantment if he wasn't marrying Aurelia."

Delphie had thought about that. "All we have to do is say that the new princess will only marry him if she can have a sunny day for her wedding."

"It's a brilliant idea," said the Queen. "Although Sugar's magic only lasts a few hours – things can only be transformed for the length of a ballet, no longer."

"We'd have to be quick then," said Delphie. "And get King Rat to marry Priscilla straight away."

"That shouldn't be too hard. Everything

will be in place for the wedding," said
Aurelia. "He was going to marry *me* today.
All we need is for him to decide to marry
Priscilla instead."

"We'll have to be careful though," said
the King. "If King Rat sees Sugar and me
and the Queen and Aurelia, he's bound to
know that there's some sort of trick going
on. He's very clever."

"Well, you could all stay here and I'll go with Priscilla. I could pretend to be her assistant." Said Delphie. "You don't think King Rat would recognise me from the time I helped the Nutcracker escape, do you?"

"Oh no, King Rat may be clever, but his memory is terrible!" Sugar replied. "I think it's a wonderful idea, Delphie."

"And I could fly on ahead and spread the news that a mysterious princess is coming," chirruped Skye. "A princess who *everyone* wants to marry."

"It might really work!" said Sugar in delight.

Delphie grinned at everyone. She loved the thought of tricking King Rat. "Then let's do it!" she cried.

A Toad in Disguise

It wasn't long before Priscilla was fetched in from the moat. She sat in the hall, looking crossly at them all, her dark eyes glaring out from her brown and green bobbly, wrinkly skin.

"This is going to take quite a lot of magic," Sugar said with a sigh.

Delphie giggled. It was very funny to

think of King Rat marrying Priscilla. They'd explained to the toad what was going to happen and all she had done was croak grumpily.

Sugar pulled a wand out of her tutu, stretched her right leg forward and then rose on to her pointes, closing her left foot neatly. Music magically swelled out into the room as Sugar swept forward. She pirouetted round Priscilla and then jumped into the air, one arm held to the side, the other above her head as she flew into the air. She landed lightly and danced on.

Delphie's feet tingled. As she watched Sugar dance, she almost felt as if she was doing the steps herself, as if *she* was the one

spinning and leaping, keeping every
movement light and delicate, her head
poised, her arms outstretched.

The music rose in volume. Sugar stopped
with one leg lifted and bent behind her, her
right hand pointing her wand at Priscilla.

There was a flash and a cloud of lilac smoke. As the smoke cleared, the music stopped and Delphie gasped. Priscilla was still in front of them but she wasn't a toad anymore. She was a beautiful brown-haired princess with enormous dark eyes. She was wearing a moss green and yellow dress, which sparkled with jewels. A heavily embroidered cloak hung from her shoulders and she was wearing a tiara with a gold veil that trailed behind her to the ground.

"Oh wow," Delphie breathed.

The King, Queen and Princess all clapped.

The toad princess's tongue shot out and she caught a fly.

Sugar giggled and came down off her pointes and dropped into a graceful curtsey. "I am pleased to present Princess Priscilla from the mysterious land of Toadonia," she said, with a grin. "And now all the princess needs is a horse-drawn sleigh!"

A little while later, Delphie sat on the front seat of a beautiful silver sleigh that was being pulled by two white horses that Sugar had conjured up from a pumpkin and two white mice just like in *Cinderella*.

The horses had green and gold plumes on their harnesses and gold bells hung from the leather reins. Griff was driving. Priscilla sat behind Delphie, a white fur rug across her knees. She looked so beautiful, it was almost impossible to believe she was the toad until she opened her mouth and a croak came out.

Even Sugar's magic couldn't make her speak!

"I think I'll have to put a spell on her so she stays silent," said Sugar, shaking her head as Priscilla croaked again. Sugar turned a pirouette and pointed her wand. Priscilla opened her mouth but no sound came out. The toad princess looked very surprised.

"Here, Priscilla," Sugar said. She magicked a bag of dried flies and handed them to the toad. "You can have these to make up for not being able to speak." Sugar looked at Delphie. "You'd better get going."

"OK! See you later!" Delphie said, pulling the warm rugs around her.

And so the sleigh set off. As the horses cantered away, their hooves sent up clouds of sparkling snow and their breath looked like steam in the frosty air. The wind rushed through Delphie's hair and she laughed in delight as Griff urged the horses on and the countryside raced by.

About twenty minutes later, a dark castle loomed up in the distance. "King Rat's castle," Delphie breathed, remembering it from before. She wondered if Skye had got there and passed around the news about the princess. She didn't have long to wait to find out.

Six of King Rat's mouse guards were standing on the roadside, dressed in leather waistcoats with swords hanging from their belts. They were each as tall as Delphie. One of them stepped out into the road and held up his paw, bringing the sleigh to a halt. "Who are you?" he called. "Declare your names!"

Delphie's heart beat faster as she stood up in the sleigh. Would they believe her? What if they realised it was all a trick? Their swords looked very sharp. She took a deep breath and hoped her voice wouldn't shake. "This is Princess Priscilla of Toadonia!" she declared. "And I am her Royal Assistant."

One of the guards, a tall skinny brown mouse, pushed his way past the guard at the front. "King Rat has heard about the Princess. Is it true she's the most beautiful princess in the whole of Enchantia?"

So Skye *had* been there spreading the word!

"It's absolutely true," Delphie declared. She swept Priscilla's veil back. The guards' eyes widened. Priscilla really did look beautiful.

"The princess is looking for a husband," Delphie told the guards. "There are many lords and princes who want to marry her. But she has heard about King Rat and she believes that he might be her perfect match. Take us to him!" she instructed grandly.

To her delight, the guards swung round. "Follow us!" said the lead guard and dropping down on to all four feet, the guards scampered off down the road.

Delphie heard King Rat before she saw him, coming from one of the open first floor windows.

"Where is this Princess?" he was shouting in his harsh voice. "I want to see her. She can't be more beautiful than Aurelia. She…" He stopped as if someone had just spoken to him. "What?" he said sharply. "She's here?"

King Rat suddenly appeared at the window. Delphie gulped. He looked just as frightening as she remembered him.

His nose was pointed, his whiskers were long and sharp, and his beady eyes gleamed red. He was wearing a spiky gold crown and a long gold cloak and was staring at Delphie. "Well, *she's* not very beautiful," he began, pointing at her. "She's just a child and rather a small one at that…"

"I'm not the princess!" Delphie stepped to one side to display the newly transformed princess. King Rat looked at Priscilla. For a moment he didn't say anything and then a smile crossed his face. "Now, she *is* beautiful!"

Priscilla opened her mouth but no sound came out.

"What's she saying? What's she saying?" demanded King Rat. He preened his whiskers.

"And what does she think of me?"

Delphie cleared her throat. "The Princess has a sore throat at the moment and can only whisper." She bent towards the toad princess and nodded as if Priscilla was talking to her. "King Rat, my princess says she has never seen such a fine figure as you, your majesty. She compliments you on your... your..." Delphie racked her brain. "On your wonderfully curling whiskers," she invented, "and your very shiny fur! She would just *love* to be your wife!"

King Rat smoothed his paw over his greasy fur. "Well, of course, people do say I am very handsome," he said haughtily. "And she is certainly more beautiful than that Princess Aurelia." He leaned out of the window. "Very well. I *will* marry you, Princess!" he called to Priscilla as if he was doing her a huge favour. "I will marry you – today!"

Delphie grinned at Griff. This was going well! "The Princess is very pleased," she told King Rat. "But she says she will only get married on a sunny day."

"But that means I would have to take my spell off Enchantia," King Rat frowned.

Delphie bent towards Priscilla and then looked at King Rat again. "The Princess will certainly not get married in the wintertime."

"Oh very well," King Rat said, looking at the princess. "Just for you, I will break the spell."

"Now?" said Delphie hopefully.

"Now!" declared King Rat. "Well, just as soon as I have got myself ready." He blew a kiss towards Priscilla. "I will be down in a few moments, my love," he said, pulling his lips back and revealing his pointed teeth in what he obviously thought was a charming smile.

As he disappeared into the castle, Delphie breathed a sigh of relief.

"It's worked!" said Griff in a low voice, and Skye twittered in delight.

Patiently they waited as King Rat stomped around, shouting at his servants. "Get me my biggest crown! No, not that one, you idiot! The one with the rubies in. I must look my very best for my bride!"

"I hope it doesn't take him *too* long to get ready," Delphie hissed to Skye and Griff.

The minutes ticked by. At long last there was a blast of trumpets. The great wooden door of the castle was thrown open and

King Rat came marching out. He stopped
and threw his arms open, as if expecting a
round of applause.

There was a moment's silence. King Rat
started to frown and then his guards
realised what he was waiting for and
hastily began to clap.

Delphie only just stopped herself from giggling. The King's whiskers had been tightly curled, and he had put oil on his greasy fur so it was slicked back and gleaming. Looking very pleased with himself, he preened vainly. "Well?" he called, looking at Delphie. "What does my princess think?"

Delphie looked round at Priscilla, preparing to make something up. She froze. Priscilla's face was turning brown and green and wrinkly. King Rat had taken so long getting ready that Sugar's magic was wearing off. Priscilla was turning back into a toad!

In Trouble

Delphie felt as if a bucket of cold, icy water had just been tipped all over her. What was she going to do now? She leapt forward and hastily pulled the veil over Priscilla's face, feeling very relieved that King Rat was so busy posing that he wasn't looking too closely at his bride-to-be.

From under the veil came a croak.

"What's that awful noise?" asked King Rat.

"Just the princess coughing," said Delphie hastily. "Coughing and saying how much she... um... she loves your curling whiskers."

King Rat smirked. "Of course she does."

There was another croak – even louder this time.

"And she *really* loves your shiny fur," Delphie babbled, trying to drown the sound. "But she says she'll only marry you if you're wearing a crown with emeralds, not rubies."

King Rat looked thoughtful. "I suppose emeralds would bring out the colour of my teeth. Very well, wait inside the hall while I get my spare crown." And with that, he hurried back into the castle.

Griff drove the sleigh as close as he could to the castle door and then jumped down as he and Delphie helped Priscilla into the hall. She was getting shorter and squatter by the moment. In just a few minutes she would have turned completely into a toad!

"Oh no, what are we going to do?"
Delphie gasped as soon as Griff had shut
the door behind them. She looked
anxiously at the staircase where King Rat
had gone.

"If only Sugar were
here," said Skye. "She
could do the dance
again and turn Priscilla back.

Delphie looked thoughtfully at the
bluebird. "Does it *have* to be Sugar who
does the dance?"

The bluebird shook her head. "No, in
Enchantia, magic comes from the dance
itself."

"Then maybe I could do the dance?"
Delphie gasped.

Just then, King Rat's voice called down
the stairs. "I'll be down in a minute, my love!"

"There isn't a moment to lose!" said Griff.
"Quick, Delphie! Please try!"

"I won't be able to do it exactly," Delphie
said hurriedly. "Because I can't dance on my
pointes yet. But I can have a go!" She took a
deep breath. Could she remember what
Sugar had done? She thought she could. Her
feet started to tingle in the red ballet shoes.

Sweeping her arms up, she rose on to her
demi-pointes. She remembered what Sugar
had done and danced forward, her arms
stretched out, her head up, hearing the
music in her head. She moved into a
pirouette, danced forward again and then
leapt into the air just as Sugar had done.

She couldn't quite manage it but she jumped as high and gracefully as she could before landing lightly. Bringing her right leg round, she stepped on to her right foot and lifted her left leg high behind her, pointing her hand at Priscilla just as Sugar had done. Delphie held her breath. Would her dancing have been good enough?

There was a flash of light and Priscilla changed back to a princess!

Skye gave a loud chirrup of excitement. The dance had worked!

"Well done, Delphie!" said Griff in delight.

Delphie ran forward and threw back Priscilla's veil. The toad looked like a beautiful girl again – and just in time as King Rat came hurrying down the stairs.

"I am here, my love!" he called. He was now wearing an ornate crown with emeralds in. "Let us get married!"

"First it's got to be a sunny day," Delphie reminded him.

King Rat pulled a glass globe out of his pocket and strode outside with Delphie, Griff and Skye following him eagerly. Inside the globe, just as Skye had said, there was a little model of Enchantia. A few snowflakes were drifting around the model just as they were outside.

King Rat put the globe down in front of him and clapped his hands. "Break!" he commanded sharply. There was a loud cracking noise and the glass shattered.

Immediately, the grey clouds parted and the sun shone through. The air grew warmer, the snow on the ground began to melt, the ice on the moat cracked and the bare branches of the trees burst into green leaf.

"It's spring!" Delphie cried, looking round as the snow melted quickly and bright blue, yellow and pink flowers pushed their way up through the grass.

"Hrumph! I suppose it is," said King Rat grumpily. "Still never mind that. I am going to get married now!"

"To a toad," Delphie whispered to Griff and Skye, with a giggle.

King Rat turned round and headed back towards Priscilla. "Come along, my love. We will be married straight away."

Delphie, Griff and Skye dashed away.
The sky was blue and the sun was shining.
Birds swooped through the air, twittering
and singing. Looking at the woods,
Delphie saw brown rabbits poking their
noses out of their burrows and squirrels
appearing from holes in tree trunks.

Suddenly there was a flash of light.
Delphie blinked as Sugar, Princess Aurelia,
King Tristan and Queen Isabella appeared
at the edge of the woods.

"Delphie!" the Princess gasped, running
forward. "You've done it! You've made
King Rat break his enchantment!"

"We saw winter change to spring and knew
your plan must have worked," said Sugar.
"So I used my magic to bring us here."

"We can't thank you enough!" said King Tristan.

Delphie glowed. She was so glad she had been able to help! "I had to do the dance that you did," she told Sugar eagerly. "The magic started to fade and Priscilla began to turn back into a toad."

"You must have danced it really well to make the magic happen," said Sugar. "But if you weren't dancing on your pointes, the magic might not last as long as last time."

"I wonder just how long it will last?" Delphie said anxiously.

Suddenly there was an ear-splitting yell from inside the castle. "What? My princess is a great big, green slimy TOAD!"

Springtime!

As they looked behind them, they saw
Priscilla come hopping out of the castle.
She charged among the guards, sending
them flying as she went this way and that,
croaking. Then suddenly she spotted the
muddy waters of the moat around King
Rat's castle. Looking very happy, she gave
a loud croak and dived in.

King Rat came charging out, shaking his fist at Delphie. "You tricked me! You... you..."

Priscilla surfaced and gave a croak so loud that everyone covered their ears.

"Go away!" King Rat shouted to the toad.

Priscilla looked at him smugly and croaked even more loudly.

"I think Priscilla likes it here!" grinned Sugar. "She looks like she's going to stay!"

King Rat looked like he was about to burst with rage. "Get me some ear plugs!" he yelled at his guards. "And lock these tricksters in the dungeons!"

The guards lunged towards them.

"Hold on, everyone!" shouted Sugar, turning a pirouette.

There was a bright flash. Delphie felt herself spinning through the air. The next moment she had landed back outside the royal family's glittering marble palace along with everyone else.

"We're back!" she cried in relief.

"And we're not the only ones!" exclaimed
Sugar. "Look!" She pointed into the sky.

Delphie gasped. A flock of bluebirds was
flying towards them.

"It's my family!" chirruped Skye, racing
to meet them before disappearing joyfully
into the group.

"Thank you, Delphie," Sugar said, taking
Delphie's hands. "It's almost time for you
to go back home but we'll see you again,
I'm sure!"

Delphie didn't really want to go but
before she had a chance to feel really sad
about leaving, Sugar waved her wand.

"Let's all dance!"

Light, bright music filled the air. The Princess, the King, the Queen, Sugar and even Griff began to dance. The bluebirds swooped around them.

"Join in with us, Delphie!" Skye chirruped.

The music swept through Delphie. She danced forward, the bluebirds encircling her in a glowing cloud. Delphie copied their delicate movements, running in tiny steps on *demi-pointes*, feeling as light as a feather. She spun into a pirouette and then went forward again, stretching her arms out like wings as the bluebirds fluttered and sang about her. Delphie raised her arms above her head, reaching into the sky

towards the fluttering birds. She sprang upwards four times, crossing her feet over with every jump. The joy of dancing filled Delphie. She had never felt so light or so graceful. It was like she was a bluebird herself. Suddenly she seemed to spin faster and faster. Colours swirled round her and she was swept into the air...

The Big Audition

She landed to find herself standing in her bedroom, her head still spinning from the dance. She looked down at her ballet shoes. They glittered for a moment and then returned to their usual red colour.

Smiling, Delphie knelt down and undid the ribbons. What an amazing adventure! She put the ballet shoes on her desk and

wriggled her toes. She was tired and her
muscles ached but she felt very, very happy.

Quietly, she got into bed. As she shut her
eyes she pictured herself dancing with the
bluebirds. She hadn't worried about her
arms and her legs, she'd just listened to the
music and danced. Was that what Madame
Za-Za had meant earlier when she said it
was important not to try too hard?

Delphie snuggled down. She couldn't
wait until the audition the next day!

The music swelled out in the ballet studio.
Delphie danced forward, lost in the
sound. Madame Za-Za was watching but
Delphie was hardly aware of her teacher.

She reached up above her head and then sprang lightly upwards, landing softly through her knees each time. She spun and danced, feeling like she was back in Enchantia, dancing with the bluebirds in the sky.

As she held the final position, her eyes glanced at Madame Za-Za and she saw her teacher nod and smile…

°⊙ˑ*. ☆ °⊙ˑ*. ☆ °⊙ˑ*. ☆ °⊙ˑ*. °

Two days later, Delphie raced up the steps into the ballet school. "Delphie!" her friend Lola said, running to meet her. "The cast list is up for the show!"

"Where?" Delphie gasped.

"It's outside Madame Za-Za's office!" Lola's eyes shone. "Oh, Delphie. I'm a robin, Poppy's a deer and you're the…"

Delphie didn't hear any more. She was already racing to the door at the end of the corridor. A piece of white paper was pinned up with the characters and

next to them the name of the person playing
that character.

Delphie's eyes found the first line:

The Bluebird... Delphie Durand.

Delphie could hardly believe it.

"It's brilliant you're the Bluebird,
Delphie!" Lola said, running up behind her.

"Look! Sukie's the rabbit!" Lola giggled.
"She's *so* not going to be happy about that!"

Delphie didn't care what part Sukie had. All that mattered was that she had danced for joy in the audition and that she owned a pair of magic ballet shoes. She turned a pirouette in delight. *What could be better than that?*

*Tiptoe over the page to learn
a special dance step...*

Darcey's Magical Masterclass

Delphie's *Demi-Plié*

*Try one of Delphie's favourite ballet moves,
a demi-plié. It's one of the first steps
that ballet dancers learn...*

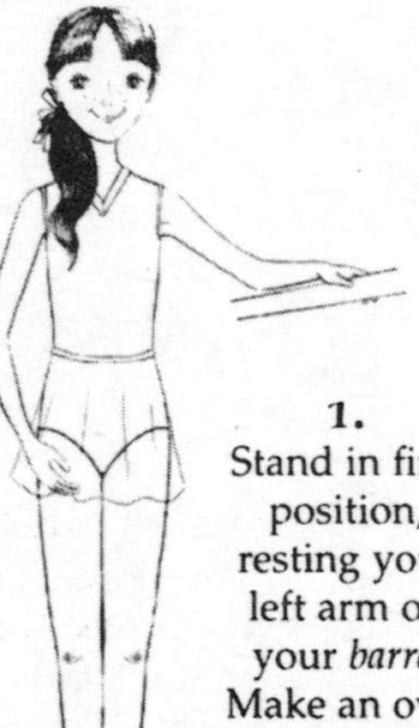

1.
Stand in first
position,
resting your
left arm on
your *barre*.
Make an oval
shape with
your right arm.

2.
Bend your
knees, keeping
your heels
together. Make
sure they don't
leave the
ground!

3.
Raise your
right arm up
in a soft curve.

4.
Now straighten
your knees and
lower your arm
gently, until you
are back in your
original position.

(P.S. Not everyone has a
barre, so you could rest
your hand on a wall or
fence instead.)

Magic
Ballerina™
Delphie and the Masked Ball

Delphie is really excited about the end of term ballet show. But while she is waiting in the wings, her help is needed in the magical world of Enchantia. Can she get there in time to save the masked ball?

Read on for a sneak preview of Delphie and the Masked Ball...

⋆ ☆ ⋆ ☆ ⋆ ☆ ⋆

Delphie landed with a bump and looked about, expecting to find herself in the theatre again, but instead she was in a large round bedroom that had a four-poster bed and a white fluffy rug on the floor.

"Delphie!"

A beautiful girl with long brown hair came hurrying over from the doorway, her hands outstretched in greeting. "Princess Aurelia!" Delphie gasped.

"What's the matter?" Delphie asked the princess, "Is it King Rat again?"

"Yes. Oh, Delphie, look!" Aurelia pointed out of the window.

Delphie turned around. What she saw made her stare. The beautiful palace courtyard below was full of animals and birds — cats, dogs, horses, deer, goats and birds of all different colours.

"What's happening? Why are there so many animals in the palace?" Delphie asked in astonishment.

"They aren't animals," Aurelia said miserably. "They're my parents' friends! King Rat has changed them all – perhaps forever!"

☆ ⋆ ☆ ⋆ ☆ ⋆ ☆ ⋆

Magic Ballerina™

Rosa and the Golden Bird

Darcey Bussell

ENCH

Royal Palace

Sugar Plum Fairy's Cottage

The Village

The Land of SWEETS

THEATRE

Theatre

*To Phoebe and Zoe, as they are the inspiration
behind Magic Ballerina.*

Contents

Prologue

In the soft, pale light, the girl stood
with her head bent and her hands
held lightly in front of her.
There was a moment's silence and then
the first notes of the music began.
For as long as the girl could remember
music had seemed to tell her of
another world – a magical, exciting
world – that lay far, far away.
She always felt if she could just
close her eyes and lose herself,
then she would get there.
Maybe this time. As the music
swirled inside her, she swept
her arms above her head, rose on to
her toes and began to dance…

At the Theatre

Rosa Maitland sat in the darkened theatre, her eyes fixed on the stage as Cinderella and Prince Charming danced together. Cinderella spun round, moving lightly across the stage. The Prince leaped into the air before sweeping her into an embrace.

Rosa glanced at her mother sitting beside

her in her wheelchair. There was a wistful look on her mum's face and Rosa wondered if she was remembering when she had once been a ballerina and danced in theatres around the world, before she'd had the accident which had ended her dancing career.

"Isn't this brilliant?" whispered Olivia, Rosa's best friend, from the seat the other side.

Rosa nodded. It was the best birthday treat ever! Her mum had got the three of them tickets to see the Petrovski Ballet Company. Rosa watched as the Prince spun Cinderella round for a final time and then Cinderella curtseyed and everyone in the audience broke into a storm of applause.

One day that will be me! Rosa thought, clapping as hard as she could. She loved dancing and went to classes three times a week at Madame Za-Za's ballet school. Her mum helped her practise between classes too.

And Rosa didn't just dance in class and at home. She had a secret. She had a pair of red ballet shoes that were magic and whisked her away to the land of Enchantia,

a place where all the characters from the
ballets lived. Rosa had had an amazing
adventure there recently and she really
hoped she would go back again soon.

As the curtain fell for the last time, lights
came up in the auditorium and one of the
theatre staff came to help Rosa's mum get
her wheelchair out. All around them people
started to stand up.

"That was amazing!" Olivia said as they
all went out into the foyer. "Thank you so
much for bringing me."

Rosa's mother smiled. "It's a pleasure,
Olivia. They're a wonderful dance
company. Their choreographer is Mikhail
Gorbachevski. I danced with him many
years ago."

"Really!" Olivia's eyes were wide. "Wow!"

"I'll show you both some pictures when we get home," said Mrs Maitland. "But first let's find a taxi."

Just as they reached the door of the theatre, Rosa heard someone call her mum's name in a Russian accent. "Eleanore! Eleanore Maitland!"

Her mum looked round.

A tall, slim man with dark hair and a grey jacket was coming towards them through the crowds.

Rosa's mother gasped. "Mikhail!"

The man took her hands and kissed her on both cheeks. "How wonderful to see you, Eleanore."

"And you." Rosa's mother smiled. "Girls, this is Mikhail who I was just telling you about." She turned back to the man. "Mikhail, this is my daughter, Rosa, and her friend, Olivia."

"Your daughter." Mikhail's eyes swept over Rosa. "She looks like you, Eleanore." He smiled at both the girls. "Did you enjoy the ballet?"

"Oh yes!" Rosa exclaimed. "It was brilliant!"

Olivia just nodded, seemingly lost for words at meeting such a famous ballet star.

"I want to be a ballerina one day," Rosa told him.

Mikhail smiled at her. "Then I hope you are as talented as your mother. Maybe you will dance for me one day." He looked at Mrs Maitland. "I would love to stay and catch up, Eleanore, but I have a meeting. Maybe you would like to bring the girls back to see *The Firebird* - the other ballet the company is performing? I can get you tickets." He pulled a wallet out of his jacket pocket and took out a card with his name and telephone number on it. "Let me know when you would like to come, and I will make sure I am free to meet up afterwards."

Rosa caught her breath. Now they would get to come to the ballet again! She turned to her mum in excitement. "Oh, wow! Wouldn't that be…"

"It's very kind of you, Mikhail," her

mum interrupted, "but I'm not sure we can manage it."

Mikhail looked surprised. "But you must."

Just then a taxi drew close. "Rosa could you get that taxi please?" Mrs Maitland said swiftly.

Wondering why her mum was being so strange, Rosa ran to ask the taxi driver to wait as her mum wheeled herself over.

"Here, let me help you," offered Mikhail as the taxi driver came round to let down a ramp to get the wheelchair into the back.

"I'll be fine, thank you," Rosa's mother said abruptly.

Mikhail's hands dropped from the chair.

The taxi driver shut the door and Mikhail came to the open window. "Goodbye, girls. Hopefully I will see you again at *The Firebird*." He looked at Rosa's mother. "Please come, Eleanore."

Mrs Maitland smiled stiffly and the taxi drove off.

"Oh, Mum! Can we go? Please!" Rosa said eagerly.

"We'll talk about it later. I'm tired." Mrs Maitland put a hand to her forehead.

Rosa sat back in her seat. *I'll talk to her tonight*, she decided. *She's got to say we can go… She's just got to!*

Enchantia Again!

"But why can't we?" Rosa demanded later that evening. Olivia had gone home and Rosa and her mum were talking about the ballet again. "Mikhail said we could have free tickets. You wouldn't have to pay."

"It's not about the money, Rosa," Mrs Maitland said briefly, busying herself in the kitchen with the washing up.

"So what is it about?" Rosa frowned, as her mum picked up a tea towel and started to dry the dishes.

She sighed. "It's complicated, sweetheart. I haven't kept in touch with any of my dancing friends because I don't want them pitying me for not being able to dance when I don't pity myself. You see, I think of all the good things that have happened since the accident – like having you. But they wouldn't see it like that and I don't want free tickets because they feel sorry for me."

Rosa thought about the man they had met at the theatre. "But Mikhail didn't seem to be offering you tickets because he felt sorry for you. He just said he wanted a chance to meet up."

"That may be what he said," Rosa's mother said, "but I think he felt differently." She sighed. "Look, it's late. Go and get ready for bed. I'm not going to talk about it any more."

Rosa couldn't believe her mum was going to turn the offer of tickets down because of this. "But Mum, what if Mikhail was just being nice and did just want to see you!" she said in frustration.

"Bed, Rosa!" her mum said.

Rosa knew that when her mum spoke that firmly there was no point arguing and so she turned and left the room. As she reached the door she glanced back. Her mum was staring at Mikhail's card, turning it over in her hand.

That night in bed, Rosa opened her *Stories from the Ballet* book and turned to the chapter on *The Firebird*. The ballet was about a princess who had been imprisoned by a magician. Whenever anyone tried to rescue her, the magician turned them to stone. But then one day a prince came along with a magical feather from a firebird which he used to rescue the princess and

turn the stone statues back into people.
Rosa shut her eyes, imagining what it
would be like to watch someone dance the
part of the Firebird...

She drifted off to sleep, dreaming of
fantastic birds and stone statues. When she
woke up a little while later, it was dark and
there was a faint tinkling sound as if

someone was playing a piano very softly.
Where was it coming from?

She sat up in bed and gasped. The red
ballet shoes at the bottom of
her bed were sparkling!
Rosa leaped up. This
must mean she was going
to Enchantia again! She pulled
on the shoes excitedly. Who would she
meet this time? What would she do?

As she tied the last ribbon, colours
started to whirl around her. She felt herself
spinning round and round, lifting into the
air.

After a few moments later she landed
back on the ground. The sparkles cleared
and the music stopped.

Rosa was standing in a wood. She could see the Royal Palace through the trees. There were butterflies flying around, rabbits hopping about and squirrels running up tree trunks. She spun round in excitement and then stopped. Something wasn't quite right. She looked around. What was it?

Suddenly she realised that there were no birds singing. The woods were silent. *That's weird*, she thought.

She looked at the palace in the distance. The last time she'd come to Enchantia she'd met Nutmeg, a helpful fairy. Maybe she should go to the palace and see if Nutmeg was there with the King and Queen.

Rosa set off. After she had been walking for about five minutes she heard the sound of voices carrying through the still air. They were raised and angry. Through the trees, she saw a small group of people. One of them was a slim fairy in a pale pink and brown tutu. *Nutmeg!*

Rosa's heart leaped at the sight of her

friend. She began to run but as she got closer, she saw that the group were arguing with a large fairy wearing a black dress and a long cloak. Her grey hair was in a bun and she had a hooked nose and warts. She looked very scary. Rosa stopped at the edge of the clearing.

"Please let the Firebird go," one of the men in the group was pleading with her.

"No!" snapped the fairy.

"But you can't just keep him in a cage. It's mean and the birds in the forest need to be able to sing again!" said Nutmeg. "You have to release him!"

The fairy glared at her. "*Have* to! No one tells me *I* have to do anything. I will do exactly as I please!"

"No you won't!" cried Nutmeg. She stepped forward towards the fairy. "We'll stop you!"

"Oh you will, will you? Well, we'll soon see about that!" The fairy laughed, a sound like breaking glass. "You impudent little fool! How dare you speak to me like that!"

She waved her long black wand. There was a flash of light and a loud crack.

Rosa's hands flew to her mouth. The people in front of the fairy were suddenly as still as statues. She had turned them all to stone!

The Fairy's Plan

The fairy threw her head back and laughed triumphantly. "I told you that you couldn't stop me!" And with that, she disappeared in a flash of green smoke.

Rosa ran into the clearing, her heart pounding.

"Nutmeg?" Rosa whispered, touching her friend's cold *grey* hand. "Nutmeg, are you OK?" But Nutmeg's face was frozen in a shocked expression.

Tears welled up in Rosa's eyes. She couldn't believe what had just happened. Nutmeg had been turned to stone! Who was the horrid fairy? What had everyone been arguing with her about?

There's something going on in Enchantia and the shoes must have brought me here to help, thought Rosa.

"I'll go to the palace straight away," Rosa told Nutmeg, in case the fairy could still hear her. She squeezed

Nutmeg's stone fingers. "Don't worry. I'll
try and sort this out. I promise!"

Running through the trees as fast as she
could, she set off towards the Royal Palace.
She headed down the main forest path until
the trees came to an end. The palace was
close by now. She raced towards the gates.

"Rosa!" the guard called. "The King and Queen were hoping you would come!"

He quickly let her in and showed her up to the royal parlour.

"Oh, Rosa! We're so glad to see you!" Queen Isabella exclaimed. She was sitting on the edge of the sofa, wringing her hands while King Tristan paced up and down.

"Enchantia is in desperate trouble," said the King.

"I saw a horrible fairy in the wood!" gasped Rosa. "She turned people to stone. Including Nutmeg!" She told the King and Queen what she had seen.

"That was the Wicked Fairy," said the King. "The same Wicked Fairy who once made our daughter, Princess Aurelia, prick her finger on a spinning wheel and fall asleep. Delphie helped to save her."

"The Wicked Fairy is horrible," said the Queen. "All the trouble at the moment is down to her."

"Why? What's going on?" burst out Rosa.

"The Wicked Fairy wants her palace to be the most talked about castle in the whole of Enchantia," King Tristan explained. "So she's been hanging cages filled with birds all around it. She sets traps and captures as many of them as she can – finches, robins, bluebirds, thrushes..."

"But the birds refused to sing in captivity," the Queen put in. "The Wicked Fairy got very angry and said that if they wouldn't sing for her then no one else

would hear any birds anywhere. So she captured the Firebird. He's part of the magic here. As long as he is free, the birds can sing and music can be played but when he is imprisoned, his magic fades so all the song and music in the land fades too."

"She's keeping him in a cage at the top of the tallest tree in Enchantia," said King Tristan. "Many brave people have tried to reach him or reason with her but she just turns them all to stone."

Just like the magician in the ballet of The Firebird, Rosa thought in alarm.

"We don't know what to do," the King went on worriedly. "There's a legend that says that if the Firebird is trapped but someone can get a feather from his tail and dance with it then he will be freed, but right now even if someone could get a feather it wouldn't be much use."

"Music and dance are linked in Enchantia," Queen Isabella explained. "Without music we simply can't dance. Look!" the Queen stood up and tried to pirouette forward, but she just stumbled and lost her balance. "Now the music has faded no one here is able to dance at all!"

Rosa frowned, remembering how she had twirled round in the woods when she had first got there. "That's strange. I think *I* can

still dance." She stood up and ran five tiny steps forward before pirouetting and then standing on one leg. She balanced perfectly.

The King and Queen gasped.

"Perhaps it's because I'm not actually from Enchantia," said Rosa. A thought suddenly struck her. "If I can get a feather from the Firebird and dance with it, then he will be free." She looked at them in excitement. "Where is he?"

"He's near the Wicked Fairy's palace which is a carriage ride away," said the King.

"It would be very dangerous to go there – the Wicked Fairy might turn you to stone!" said the Queen.

"I'll risk it!" Rosa said bravely.

"Oh, Rosa, I really don't know," said Queen Isabella worriedly.

"I must!" said Rosa. "The shoes have brought me here so I can help. I have to go. If you won't lend me a carriage, I'll just set off on my own!"

The King hesitated and then nodded. "Rosa has clearly made up her mind," he said, taking his wife's hand. "Let us at least give her what protection we can." He turned to Rosa. "If you are sure you want to go, I will call you a carriage and driver straight away."

Rosa lifted her chin. "I do. I want to go. I'm going to free the Firebird and save Enchantia. The Wicked Fairy isn't going to stop me!"

Traps in the Trees

It was getting chilly as Rosa pulled the rugs in the carriage around her. Now the journey had started she began to wonder how it was going to end. How *was* she going to rescue the Firebird? What if she met the Wicked Fairy and was turned to stone like everyone else?

A picture of the Wicked Fairy's pale face

swam into Rosa's head and she shivered.
She had felt so brave back at the palace, but
now she could feel doubts filling her mind.
What if I can't help this time? she thought
anxiously. *What if I fail? How am I going to
get a feather from the Firebird's tail?*

The driver – Griff – looked over his
shoulder at her. "I used to know Delphie,
the girl who had the ballet shoes before
you," he said.

Rosa smiled. He was talking about
Delphie Durand – the dark-haired girl at
Madame Za-Za's ballet school who had
given Rosa the red ballet shoes when she
could no longer wear them.

"She's one of my friends," Rosa smiled.
"She's really nice, isn't she?"

"Oh yes," Griff said. "Nice and brave. And such a lovely girl. It always seemed like she could solve every problem."

Rosa swallowed. *Delphie would have thought of a plan by now*, she thought.

"She always came up with some idea that could help," Griff went on. "So what's your plan for rescuing the Firebird then?"

"I'm… I'm not sure," Rosa admitted, feeling like a bit of a let down.

"Oh." Griff looked a bit surprised but then shrugged. "Well, I'm sure you'll think of something by the time we get there."

He turned back to look at the horses. *He's probably wishing Delphie was here instead of me,* thought Rosa. Pulling the rug around her, she stared at the countryside whizzing past. She hoped she'd think of something soon!

°⊙·*·☆·⊙·*·☆·⊙·*·☆·⊙·*·°

The horses cantered past fields and villages till at last they reached a wood of tall trees. There, Rosa could see strange wooden contraptions, like cages, made from branches. "What are they?" she asked.

"They're the bird traps set by the Wicked Fairy," Griff said grimly. "She's captured

most of the birds in this wood already." The
horses shook their heads nervously.

Rosa stared at the empty cages, thinking
of all the birds the Wicked Fairy had
captured and hoping no more would be
caught. Suddenly her eyes were caught by a
flash of blue in a cage halfway up a tree to
her left. "Look!"

"It's a bird," Griff slowed the horses and
peered through the trees. "A bluebird by
the looks of it."

"We've got to let it out!" said Rosa.
"What if the Wicked Fairy comes and takes
it?"

"What if she comes and sees us here?"
said Griff doubtfully. "If a bird is caught
that probably means she'll be along soon
to check the traps. We should get on our
way."

But Rosa stood up. "No! I'm getting out!
I'm going to rescue it!"

Almost before Griff had halted the
horses, Rosa had scrambled down from the
carriage. She hurried off the path, jumping
over tree roots and ducking under branches
until she reached the tree. A small bluebird
with turquoise feathers and shining
dark eyes was trapped inside the cage.

"Help!" he called, flapping his wings in alarm.

"Don't worry," called Rosa. "I'm coming!" She started to climb the tree, standing on tiptoe to grab the lowest branch with both hands and pulling herself up. Once on that branch she climbed up to another and another.

She looked at the door of the cage. It was fiddly to undo – a bird would never be able to manage it with its beak, but she could just about do it with her fingers – and pulled it open.

The bird opened its mouth, as if about to sing in delight, but no song came out. Instead, he swooped out and perched on her shoulder. "Oh, thank you! Thank you!" He butted his little head against her cheek. "I know I should never have flown into the woods but I was chasing a flying bug for my tea. I didn't see the cage until I flew inside. The door shut behind me and then I was trapped."

Rosa stroked his head. "You'd better get out of here. Just watch out for other traps on the way!"

She began to climb down the tree. The little bird flew after her. "My name's Skye."

"I'm Rosa."

"It's lovely to meet you, Rosa. I met Delphie once," said Skye. "She's lovely. So brave!"

There it was again – that same word. *Brave.* Rosa bit her lip. She wished people would stop telling her how amazing Delphie was. It wasn't making her feel very good by comparison.

"Are you going to rescue the Firebird?" Skye asked. "Can I come with you?"

"Thanks but I'd better go on my own. It'll be really dangerous," said Rosa.

"I don't mind," cheeped Skye. "I'd like to come and help."

"No," Rosa insisted. She would have loved the little bird's company, but what if they met the Wicked Fairy and he was caught? "You should get out of here. Go somewhere safe."

"But…"

"Rosa! We should go!" Griff called to her.

"Coming! Bye, Skye!" Rosa ran back to the carriage, waving back to the little bluebird. "Watch out for those cages!"

"But… but…" the little bird twittered.

Griff brought the reins down on the horses' backs and they leaped forward. "We'd best be off. It's too dangerous to stay here and the Firebird needs to be freed," he said.

Rosa felt as if Griff was telling her off for stopping to rescue Skye. *He probably thinks Delphie wouldn't have stopped*, she thought. Sighing, she pulled the rugs up around her and set her mind to thinking what she would do to free the Firebird. She had to think of something – and fast!

In the Clearing

The rest of the journey passed in silence. A few times Rosa saw Griff start to turn towards her but she hastily shut her eyes as if she was dozing. She didn't want him starting to tell her how amazing he thought Delphie was again, particularly seeing as she was aware that she still hadn't thought of a plan!

She kept wracking her brains. How was she going to get up to its cage? What was she going to do if the Wicked Fairy was there?

She caught sight of a palace through the trees. It was made of grey stone and had black flags flying from its pointed turrets. All around it were cages full of birds.

Griff slowed the horses to a walk. "The tallest tree is close to the edge of the woods," he said. "It might be safer to walk the last bit in case the Wicked Fairy hears the horses coming."

Rosa swallowed nervously. This was it. They were here. Griff halted and she got down. There was a clearing a little way ahead of them, and in it were six stone statues, two princes on horses, a fairy, a girl dressed as a soldier and two princes on foot.

They must all be people who had tried to rescue the Firebird! She started to hurry towards the clearing.

"Be careful, Rosa!" Griff called in a low voice.

But Rosa ignored him. She wanted to get to the Firebird as quickly as possible. But, just as she reached the edge of the clearing, the Wicked Fairy appeared ahead of her!

Just in time, Rosa threw herself down behind a leafy bush. The Wicked Fairy swung around and looked suspiciously in her direction, as if she had heard a noise.

With her heart beating fast, Rosa realised that the bush was hollow in the middle. She quickly crawled inside, hoping Griff was hiding too. Branches caught in her hair and her fingernails dug into the soil but she took no notice. Her eyes were fixed on the Wicked Fairy who was stalking straight towards her!

As the Wicked Fairy reached the bush where she was hiding, Rosa hardly dared to breathe. *Please don't see me*, she thought. *Please!*

"Must just have been a bird," the Wicked Fairy muttered, cackling. "If it is, I'll catch it for my collection!" She marched back into the clearing and looked up towards something in the branches of one of the trees. "How are you enjoying your cage, Firebird?" she called out. "Get used to it because you'll be staying there for a long time!" And with that, she waved her wand and vanished in a flash.

Phew! thought Rosa as she crawled out from under the bush.

"Rosa, are you OK?"

She looked round and saw Griff coming out from behind a tree trunk. "You shouldn't have run ahead like that! You could have been caught!"

"I know, it was stupid!" The scare she had just had made Rosa speak more crossly than she would usually. "I bet Delphie would never have done anything like that, would she?"

Griff stared at her. "What do you mean?"

All the worry about not having thought of a plan yet and the fear that she wasn't as good as Delphie, spilled out of Rosa. "Well, it's clear you think Delphie would have been more careful and that Delphie would have had a plan. You think she was *wonderful!*"

Griff looked astonished. "Yes, she was. But so are you. I've heard about your last adventure here and how you got into King  Rat's castle. That was incredible. And the way you insisted on rescuing Skye the bluebird. That was really brave too." He frowned. "I've only been talking about Delphie because I really liked her and you said you were friends. I didn't mean to make it sound like Delphie was braver or better than you."

"Oh." Rosa went red as she realised that she had jumped to conclusions.

Griff looked upset.

Rosa swallowed, feeling bad for upsetting him. "I'm… I'm sorry," she said. "I got it wrong. I should have asked you what you meant."

Griff gave her a kindly smile. "That's all right. We both just got our wires crossed. Let's forget it now. There are far more important things to think about – like how to rescue the Firebird before the Wicked Fairy comes back. Look, there he is!"

Griff pointed up the tallest tree. A handsome prince had been turned to stone

right beside it, looking up into the branches.
Rosa saw a narrow cage hanging near the
very top. A bird about the size of an eagle
was shut inside.
It had beautiful
red and gold
feathers and a
proud face.

"The Firebird!"
Rosa breathed.

"He shouldn't
be trapped like
that. He should be
free," said Griff, stepping over a pile of
cloaks that had been discarded by people
as they had got ready to rescue the
Firebird.

"How are you going to get up there?" he said, walking up to the tree. "It looks impossible!"

Rosa remembered how she had just saved Skye. "I'll climb up."

"But there aren't any branches you can reach from here," Griff pointed out.

Rosa realised he was right. The lower part of the trunk was very smooth. The first branches were far out of reach, about five metres up the tree. It would be impossible to climb from the ground.

"If only we had a ladder," she said, looking around the clearing.

But there was nothing around that could help. Unless…

Her eyes fell on the statue of the prince near the trunk and widened as she thought of an idea. "Griff, could you climb on that statue? Then, if I climb up on your shoulders, I should be able to reach the first branch!"

Griff looked at the stone statue and then looked at the branches. "Yes, I could do that. I'm sure Prince Hugo wouldn't mind."

"I'm sorry, Prince Hugo," Rosa said quickly to the prince in case he could hear. It wasn't very dignified for a prince to be climbed on, but they had to rescue the Firebird and this was the only way she could think of.

Griff began to climb on to the prince's shoulders.

Once he was balanced, Rosa followed him up. It was a bit like being an acrobat in the circus! Griff bent down and she climbed on to his shoulders and then he straightened slowly up. She could almost reach the lowest branch, almost…

Griff wobbled. Rosa made a desperate grab and her fingers found a branch. Using all of her strength, she hauled herself up so her tummy was on the branch, and then pulled her legs up. Taking a deep breath, she began to climb.

It was very difficult. The branches were spaced out and thoughts of the Wicked Fairy kept filling Rosa's mind. What if she came back and saw Rosa halfway up the tree? There would be no way to hide from her there.

Rosa glanced down. The ground was a long way off now. A wave of dizziness swept over her. She clutched the trunk, feeling like she was  going to fall. *Don't stop, don't stop*, she told herself. But suddenly her arms and legs felt as if they wouldn't work.

I can't do it, she thought in panic. *I can't!*

"Go on, Rosa!" urged Griff from below.

Rosa took courage from his voice. Everyone in Enchantia needed her to do this. She wasn't going to give up!

Gritting her teeth, she edged further up the tree. She'd gone a few more metres when suddenly her feet slipped. For a moment she swung in mid-air, her hands locked round a branch before she regained her footing and edged back towards the trunk to pause, trembling and clinging on.

She shut her eyes, blinking back the tears. *You have to keep going*, she told herself and taking a deep breath, she began to climb again...

Rescued!

"Rosa!"

Rosa looked round and gasped. Skye, the little bluebird, was swooping towards her.

"Skye!" she gasped. "What are you doing here? I told you not to come."

"But I thought you might need help. I tried to keep up with the carriage, but I couldn't – I needed to fly carefully because

of the traps. Anyway, I'm here now!" Skye
flew closer, his dark eyes concerned. "Are
you all right?"

"Not really," Rosa said, hanging on to the
tree trunk. "I've got to get up to the
Firebird."

The bluebird looked worried. "I could
fly up there but I won't be able to undo his
cage with my beak."

"I don't need to do undo the cage," Rosa
said quickly. "I just need one of his tail
feathers."

"I can easily get one of those for you!"
said Skye.

"Really?" said Rosa, her heart jumping.

"Of course! Watch me!" Skye flew
upwards.

Rosa watched the little bird fly all the
way to the cage. He chirruped something to
the Firebird who nodded his elegant head.
The bluebird gently
plucked one of the
red-gold feathers out of
his long tail, then
whizzed back
down to Rosa
with it.

"You've got
it!" she gasped.
She longed to take the shining feather, but
first she had to get back down the tree. She
began the long, slow climb down, her feet
slowly finding footholds, her arms trembling
with the strain.

"Rosa!" she heard Griff shout from below. "Jump!"

Rosa glanced down. Griff had made a hammock with the discarded cloaks! He had strung it between the statue of Prince Hugo and a nearby statue of a man on a horse. If she jumped, she would land in it and then she would be on the ground and could do the dance!

"Come on," urged Griff again.

"Go on, Rosa!" said Skye.

Taking a deep breath, Rosa jumped. For a few brief seconds she felt the air whizzing past, saw the blue sky overhead, and thought she was going to crash into the ground. But then she landed in the hammock. She bounced upwards and down again, as if she was on a trampoline!

She blinked as her bouncing slowed down. Griff was grinning at her.

"Thanks!" she gasped, swinging her legs over the side and tumbling out.

Skye swooped down. "Here's the feather, Rosa!"

Rosa took it gratefully and ran to the centre of the clearing. Now all she had to do was dance. But which should she perform?

Then she remembered what she had
watched the dancers doing the night before
at the theatre.

She raised her arms above her head,
crossed her left leg behind her right and
then ran forward, bringing her arms down

so they were just slightly
behind her. She
pirouetted and
danced forward
another step before
balancing on her
toes. Then she
circled round the
statues, turning with
every step, arms out
to the sides, the feather

whisking through the air. As she turned
and spun, she heard the faint sound of
birdsong! She stopped in an arabesque, one
leg out behind her and looked at Skye. The
little bird had his mouth open and notes
were starting to pour out.
He flapped his wings in
delight. "I'm singing
again!"

Rosa spun on again and suddenly music
started to fill the clearing. She got faster
and faster as the music grew louder and
stronger. Acting instinctively, she brushed
the feather against the statues. As soon as
the feather touched the first one, the stone
on all of them started to crack and they
began to turn back into real people. The

music reached a peak and there was a loud
BANG!

Rosa stopped, her gaze flying upwards.
The bottom of the cage had burst open

and the Firebird was
swooping out and
into the air, free at
last! The cage
came away from
the branch and
started to fall
when suddenly
there was a piercing,
furious shriek…

Rosa turned to see the Wicked Fairy
rushing into the clearing!

The Firebird's Feather

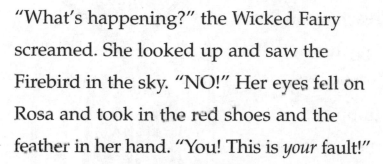

"What's happening?" the Wicked Fairy screamed. She looked up and saw the Firebird in the sky. "NO!" Her eyes fell on Rosa and took in the red shoes and the feather in her hand. "You! This is *your* fault!"

Rosa shrank back, her blood running icy with fear.

The Wicked Fairy lifted her wand. "Just you wait…"

She broke off with a shriek as the narrow
cage above her plummeted down from the
sky, falling straight over her head and
snapping her wand.

"What the… what the…" The Wicked
Fairy stared out from behind the bars. She
began to waddle
around, the cage
reaching all the
way down to her
ankles. "I'm
trapped! Get
me out of here!"
she yelled
furiously. "GET
ME OUT!"

"No way," cried Rosa.

"You trapped the Firebird in there! Now see how you like it!"

The Wicked Fairy jumped up and down with rage. But no one was about to help her.

"I'll get you all for this!" she cursed, stamping away through the trees.

"I hope no one lets her out for a while!" Prince Hugo said.

Rosa grinned. She was sure the Wicked Fairy would find someone to take the cage off her at some point but right now it was good that she had a taste of her own medicine!

The fairy who had been a statue pirouetted over to Rosa. "I'm Sugar the Sugar Plum Fairy, Nutmeg's older sister. You set the Firebird free and saved the day!" She took Rosa's hands. "Now I will use my magic to take us back to the Royal Palace. They will all be celebrating there and the King and Queen will want to know what happened!"

Rosa's eyes flew to Griff.

"Don't worry about me," he said. "I'll head back with the carriage."

"And I'm going to see if I can find my family," said Skye flying down from up on high. "I've just been above the treetops and the cages at the Wicked Fairy's palace have burst open too. All the birds are free!"

"Brilliant!" Rosa gasped. She turned to Sugar. "Yes, please take me back."

But just as Sugar raised her wand, the Firebird swooped down into the clearing in a blaze of red and gold. Every feather on his body glittered and shone with magic and his dark eyes looked brightly at Rosa. "Thank you!" he called to Rosa. "You have brought music and song back to Enchantia."

Rosa smiled in delight, watching as he flew up into the sky, soaring above the trees, free once again.

Looking happily at the feather in her hand, she slipped it into her pyjama pocket.

Sugar grinned. "Come on. Your job here is done. Let's go back to the palace!"

Sugar waved her wand. Pink sparkles swirled around Rosa and the next second she felt herself being whisked away.

Back in the palace, everyone was celebrating, just as Sugar had said. Birds were perched on every part of the palace walls, singing sweetly as if to make up for the time they had been silent. A band was playing and people were dancing in the courtyard.

"Rosa! Sugar!"

Rosa swung round and saw Nutmeg pushing her way through the crowd. "What happened? All we know is that suddenly the spell broke and everyone was free."

"Let's go inside and Rosa can tell the King and Queen too," said Sugar and they hurried into the palace.

"I'm so glad you're all right," said Rosa to Nutmeg. "I saw you being turned into stone. It was awful."

"I'm OK. It didn't hurt," said Nutmeg. "And now everyone is fine, thanks to you!"

They got inside and Rosa told the King and Queen and Nutmeg what had happened.

"I couldn't have done it without Griff and Skye," she finished.

"They will be well rewarded," the King promised. "Now, come and join the dancing outside!"

But as he spoke, Rosa's shoes started to glow. "I've got to go!" she gasped.

"See you soon, Rosa!" called Nutmeg.

"Bye!" cried Rosa as she was whisked away.

She landed back in her bedroom in the dark. What an adventure! She could hardly believe everything that had just happened.

She untied her ballet shoes and then climbed into her bed, a minute later she was fast asleep.

Second Chances

The next morning she went downstairs, her fingers playing with the Firebird feather in her pocket. Her mum was in the kitchen getting out the breakfast things. Rosa took a deep breath. "Mum, I've been thinking about the tickets and I think you should ring Mikhail."

Her mum sighed. "We went through this

last night. I'm sorry if you're disappointed, love but..."

Rosa didn't let her finish. "Mum, it's not just because I want to go and see the ballet, although of course I do. I just think you really should ring Mikhail. I know you think that he's feeling sorry for you, but sometimes," and she thought about Griff, "well, we don't always get it right when we guess what other people are thinking, and you said you and he were friends."

Rosa held her breath, wondering what her mum would say.

Her mum stared. "Where did all that come from?"

Rosa shrugged. "I don't know. I was just thinking about it. You should find out what

Mikhail's really thinking and not just guess. You're always telling me not to judge people." She looked hopefully at her mum. "Please will you ring him?"

A smile caught at her mum's mouth. "I can't argue with that. You're right. Maybe I shouldn't jump to conclusions. Perhaps I have got it wrong."

Rosa's eyes widened. "So you'll ring?"

Her mum hesitated and then nodded.

"I will. And if he offers me tickets again, I'll say yes."

Rosa spun round joyfully. She was sure her mum was just as mistaken about Mikhail as she had been about Griff. "Oh wow!" she gasped. "Just wait until I tell Olivia!"

°⊙⋅*⋅☆ ⊙⋅*⋅☆ ⊙⋅*⋅☆ ⊙⋅*⋅°

Two weeks later, Rosa sat in the auditorium of the theatre with her mum, Mikhail and Olivia. From the moment they had met up with him before the show, he and Rosa's mother had been laughing and talking, catching up on lost time. Every seat was filled. The stage was blazing with light as a dancer dressed in a red and gold costume leaped across the stage, arms thrown back like a bird in flight.

Rosa pictured the real Firebird soaring through the sky in Enchantia. When would she go back there again? She put her hand in the pocket of her skirt and her fingers closed around the feather. *Soon*, she thought. And she smiled.

The Firebird's Flight

*The Firebird is an amazing creature that flies all over Enchantia!
Try this springing step and imagine that you are the Firebird starting
to take flight, remember to flap those arms like wings!*

1.
Start in the 3rd
position, with
your left foot
behind your
right foot and
your arms in
the prepare
position.

2.
Bend your
knees.

3.
Spring your feet out to the side and rise on to demi-toes – this is called an *echappe* in ballet. Try to keep your feet as close to the ground as possible. Raise your arms as you do this as if you're flapping your wings.

4.
Stay on your demi-toes for a couple of seconds and then spring your feet back to the position that you started in, lowering your arms. Start again and repeat all the steps, until you're in full flight!

Magic
Ballerina™
Rosa and the Magic Moonstone

The magical moonstone of Enchantia has broken and all of the ballets have become muddled up! Can Rosa put things right?

Read on for a sneak preview of Rosa and the Magic Moonstone...

The air filled with music and the curtains started to open, revealing a brightly lit stage. A girl in a nightdress danced on. Maybe it's Clara from *The Nutcracker*, thought Rosa, wondering what was happening. But then she saw that the girl wasn't holding a nutcracker doll, she was holding a pumpkin! She was followed by a group of soldiers who looked like they were also from *The Nutcracker*. They were fighting a group of dancing giant sweets. *But in the ballet they fight an army of mice*, thought Rosa.

Before she had time to say anything, the soldiers had danced off the stage and a girl in rags had come on. *Cinderella!* thought Rosa. A beautiful fairy spun on after her. But it wasn't Cinderella's Fairy Godmother, it was Sugar, the Sugar Plum Fairy! Two more people followed them. They were dancing a *pas de deux*. One of them was a beautiful girl with long dark hair who looked like Sleeping Beauty. Rosa stared.

Sleeping Beauty wasn't dancing with her handsome prince though; instead she was dancing with a surprised-looking Puss In Boots!

What's going on? Rosa wondered. All the ballets seem to be completely mixed up!

The curtain started to close. Rosa jumped to her feet. "Wait!" she called. She hurried out of her row of seats. But the curtains had shut.

° ⊙ ⠄* ☆ ⠄⊙ ⠄* ☆ ⊙ ⠄* ☆ ⊙ ⠄* °

Hi, I'm Rosa. I've always loved dancing! Madame Za-Za tells me to slow down and concentrate on what I'm doing, but dancing is just so exciting. Delphie gave me the precious red ballet shoes and, before I knew it, I was in Enchantia meeting all the ballet characters. Nutmeg (Sugar's sister) and I have been on lots of adventures: rescuing an enchanted princess, finding stolen treasure and thwarting the Wicked Fairy at every turn.

Hair colour: Blonde

Eye colour: Blue

Likes: Olivia my best friend, making my mum happy

Dislikes: Making mistakes or losing my temper

Favourite ballet: Swan Lake

Best friend in Enchantia: Nutmeg

Read all my Magic Ballerina adventures...

7 Magic Ballerina
Rosa and the Secret Princess
Darcey Bussell

8 Magic Ballerina
Rosa and the Golden Bird
Darcey Bussell

9 Magic Ballerina
Rosa and the Magic Moonstone
Darcey Bussell

10 Magic Ballerina
Rosa and the Special Prize
Darcey Bussell

11 Magic Ballerina
Rosa and the Magic Dream
Darcey Bussell

12 Magic Ballerina
Rosa and the Three Wishes
Darcey Bussell

Magic Ballerina

Darcey Bussell

Buy more great Magic Ballerina books direct from HarperCollins
at 10% off recommended retail price.
FREE postage and packing in the UK.

Delphie and the Magic Ballet Shoes	ISBN 978 0 00 728607 2
Delphie and the Magic Spell	ISBN 978 0 00 728608 9
Delphie and the Masked Ball	ISBN 978 0 00 728610 2
Delphie and the Glass Slippers	ISBN 978 0 00 728617 1
Delphie and the Fairy Godmother	ISBN 978 0 00 728611 9
Delphie and the Birthday Show	ISBN 978 0 00 728612 6
Rosa and the Secret Princess	ISBN 978 0 00 730029 7
Rosa and the Golden Bird	ISBN 978 0 00 730030 3
Rosa and the Magic Moonstone	ISBN 978 0 00 730031 0
Rosa and the Special Prize	ISBN 978 0 00 730032 7
Rosa and the Magic Dream	ISBN 978 0 00 730033 4
Rosa and the Three Wishes	ISBN 978 0 00 730034 1

All priced at £3.99

To purchase by Visa/Mastercard/Maestro simply call
08707871724 or fax on **08707871725**